MR PATTACAKE
and the
DOG'S DINNER DISASTER

'Ook, Eacle,' said Mr Pattacake, hopping from one foot to the other in excitement, his big chef's hat wobbling. What he was trying to say was, 'Look, Treacle,' but he had a mouthful of cornflakes, so that's why it came out all funny. As well as the muffled words, a little spattering of cornflakes came out of his mouth too.

He waved a letter in the air while doing the silly little dance he always did when he was excited.

Treacle, his ginger cat, had to jump out of the way of his big feet. He then yawned, showing that there were no cornflakes in *his* mouth. In fact, there was nothing at all in his mouth. It was about time Mr Pattacake gave him *his* breakfast.

Treacle knew that the letter must mean a cooking job for Mr Pattacake. He was excited too, but didn't show it in the same way that his owner did. He was a quiet sort of cat, but he *did* smile to himself. When Mr Pattacake did some cooking there was always something in it for him.

'A pet food company called ANiMEALS wants me to invent some delicious new food for pets,' said Mr Pattacake, excitedly, having now swallowed his cornflakes. 'People are complaining that their pets are refusing to eat because they are bored with the same food. That's definitely a job for us, Treacle, and you can be the chief cat food taster.'

Treacle licked his lips in delight. His tummy rumbled at the very thought. That was just the kind of job he liked.

Mr Pattacake straightened his yellow and black checked waistcoat and put on his big white apron. It was time to make his to-do list.

'First we have to invent some names for the food,' he said, picking up a pen and sitting down at the table.

It didn't take him long. Mr Pattacake's imagination worked very fast.

'Listen, Treacle. What do you think? We can
have:

Dog's Dinner,

Cat's Casserole,

Rabbit's Rations,

Bird's Breakfast,

Fish's Feast,

and Snake's Supper.'

Treacle sat on a chair washing his whiskers and paused to look up briefly as Mr Pattacake finished reading out the list.

'I knew you would like them,' said Mr Pattacake, smiling at Treacle. He understood cats very well – he even knew what they were thinking.

Mr Pattacake went off in his little yellow van to buy the ingredients. Then he got to work straight away.

Soon, Mr Pattacake had six big pans bubbling on the stove. He'd put in lots of delicious things that he knew each of the pets would love – plus a sprinkling of this and a dash of that. He'd also thrown in a handful of flavouring and just a shake of his magic ingredient.

Animals were fussy – he'd owned many of them in his time. Dogs, cats, mice, rabbits, a Shetland pony, and even a pot-bellied pig. So this job was just the thing for him. He was an **EXPERT** on animals.

The Cat's Casserole took the longest time to get right because the chief cat food taster was very particular. Treacle shrugged and shook his head, and swished his tail and even hissed as he tasted Mr Pattacake's different ideas.

It was a long time before he began to purr softly with approval, and by then he hardly had the energy left because he was too full.

Some of his friends came in too and gave their opinion. As the smells wafted out into the street they brought in one or two dogs as well – Bobby, the Jack Russell, from number ten, Mrs Hall's springer spaniel, Tia, and even a few that Mr Pattacake had never seen before. A white rabbit called Snowy hopped in, and an escaped green budgie too. Soon Mr Pattacake's kitchen looked like a zoo.

'Shoo!' said Mr Pattacake, flapping his hands, and looking round to make sure there were no snakes slithering around on the floor. 'I'm trying to work here.' But the animals would not move until he had given each of them a little taste.

They chewed. They rolled their eyes. They swallowed. Then they all jumped up and down with excitement – each one gave their approval. They all thought the food was **DELICIOUS!**

Meanwhile, Mr Pattacake got out six giant plastic pots with lids, and wrote on some labels, *dog, cat, rabbit, bird, fish, snake,* which he then stuck on the lids.

Finally, Treacle politely asked the animals to leave and showed them out of the door. He and Mr Pattacake had lots to do.

But the green budgie stayed behind, eyeing Treacle from the top of the cupboard. He didn't like being told what to do, especially by a cat.

The green budgie then flew down on to the worktop. Treacle tried to ignore him, and Mr Pattacake was busy, so neither of them noticed him meddling with the pot lids.

At last he flew out of the window.

'Right,' said Mr Pattacake, picking up one of the big saucepans. 'Where is the first pot for the Dog's Dinner? All the lids are in order so you can put them on, Treacle.'

Treacle pushed a pot forward and Mr Pattacake tipped the food into it. At last, when all the pots were full, Treacle put on the lids and jumped on them to fasten them tightly.

Except…

Treacle was a cat and he couldn't read. Oh dear! What a muddle!

Mr Pattacake, unaware of the mix-up, loaded the pots into his little van and drove off to **ANiMEALS**.

Job done!

Treacle curled up in a patch of warm sunlight. He had eaten sooooo much. There was something worrying him however, but he just sighed and closed his eyes. Nothing ever worried him for long.

Mr Pattacake wasn't worrying about anything. He was thinking about the money he would make from the recipes when ANIMEALS saw how successful the food was. Pet owners would be queuing up to buy the food and he would be even more well-known than he was now.

But he waited…

And waited…

But there was no news from ANiMEALS.

What had gone wrong?

Then one day Mr Pattacake received a phone call.

'Are you Mr Pattacake? The one who made the Dog's Dinner?' asked the lady on the phone.

Ah! A satisfied customer at last, Mr Pattacake thought to himself. 'Yes, I am,' he said happily.

'You'd better come and have a look at my dog, Benny,' she said.

She didn't sound pleased at all. Whatever could be wrong?

Mr Pattacake and Treacle went round to the lady's house. Treacle normally didn't like dogs very much, but he was curious to know what was wrong, and his nagging little worry had returned.

When the lady opened the front door, Mr Pattacake looked round, expecting the dog to come running to see who it was, as dogs do.

'Oh, he's not in the house,' said the lady, shaking her head. 'It's very strange. Come and take a look.' She led them out to the back garden.

In one corner was a big fish pond.

Benny, the Labrador, was in the water. At least, Mr Pattacake assumed it was Benny. In some places where there should have been golden fur, there were pale pink scales instead. Benny was swimming around the pond, opening and closing his mouth without making a sound, and on his head sat a green frog.

'Benny!' Mr Pattacake patted his knee, trying to get him to come out of the water.

Benny's doggy side tried to wag his tail, but it was difficult to do so in the pond, so it just resulted in spraying water all over Mr Pattacake and the lady.

They both looked surprised and tried to brush the water off their clothes.

Treacle, on the other hand, being a clever cat who hated getting wet, had seen it coming and got out of the way just in time.

'He won't come out,' said the lady, frowning. She backed away from the pond a little too late. 'He loved your pet food, but I think there must have been some terrible mistake. He stays in the pond all the time now. He doesn't even want to go for walks anymore, and he's looking more and more like a fish every day.' She sounded very worried.

Mr Pattacake took off his big chef's hat and shook the water off it. Then he glared at Treacle, and Treacle felt that nagging little worry grow even bigger.

It couldn't be his fault though, could it? He was a cat, and cats couldn't read.

He hadn't been able to read the labels on the food pots, and Mr Pattacake rather foolishly hadn't checked.

'What are we going to do, Mr Pattacake?' said the lady. 'I want my lovely Benny back, not this dog fish. My nice *furry* Benny, who likes going for walks.'

'Don't worry, I'll put it right,' said Mr Pattacake, trying to sound convincing, although he wasn't exactly sure what he was going to do. He needed to get his imagination to work on it.

But before he had time to think, he received a text message.

It read:

MR PATTACAKE. WHAT DID YOU PUT IN THE CAT'S CASSEROLE? MY CAT, FLUFFY, KEEPS TRYING TO FLY.
PLEASE COME AND HELP.

Mr Pattacake gasped with horror. He was no longer his usual happy self. His big chef's hat didn't wobble with excitement anymore, but rather trembled with worry. What had gone wrong with the pets' meals?

He and Treacle got in the little yellow van and drove to the boy's house. When they arrived, a small crowd had gathered on the pavement and were all looking up, their mouths open in fear. On the edge of the roof stood a black cat, its front paws held up like wings.

'Come down, Fluffy!' the boy pleaded, his arms stretched out towards the strange creature on the roof. 'You can't fly. You're a cat.'

Fluffy was not so fluffy anymore. It was difficult to see at that height, but Mr Pattacake thought his fur looked more like feathers, and his front legs had widened to look more like wings, but not enough to make him to fly though.

Fluffy answered the boy, but instead of a meow, it was a tweet.

Now everyone knows that cats can jump from high places and always land on their feet, but this was definitely *too* high.

Just then, Mr Pattacake had one of his sudden ideas.

'I know what to do!' he shouted, trying to save the situation. 'Go and fetch a large bed sheet,' he told the boy. 'The biggest you can find!'

The boy looked doubtful, but then nodded and ran inside his house. He soon returned with an enormous white cotton sheet.

'Now,' instructed Mr Pattacake, opening the sheet out, 'everyone must take an edge of the sheet and we'll all hold it like a safety net so we can catch Fluffy.'

Everyone grabbed part of the sheet and held it out taut just in time before Fluffy spread her wing-like paws and took off from the roof.

She didn't fly of course. Despite flapping her paws rapidly, she just dropped straight down onto the sheet like a lead weight. She was so frightened that she just bounced right out again, but this time she landed perfectly on her feet on the pavement and scooted away in a flash.

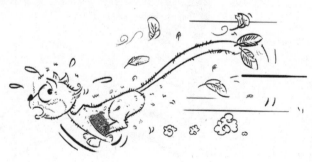

'Thank you, Mr Pattacake,' said the boy, looking relieved. 'But you'll have to do something before she tries to fly again. She will hurt herself. I want a fluffy cat, not a bird.'

'Don't worry, I'll put it right,' said Mr Pattacake, trying to sound reassuring, and he and Treacle went home so they could start thinking.

Before Mr Pattacake could begin, however, he received an email. It was from a small girl called Katy.

'Mr Pattacake. My rabbit, Bounce, loved the Rabbit Rations that you invented, but now he's not acting like a rabbit anymore.'

Once again, Mr Pattacake and Treacle set off in the little yellow van to the pet owner's house. Mr Pattacake could see that something very wrong had happened, and that this wouldn't be the end of it.

When the little girl opened the door, a rabbit came running to greet them, barking like a dog. He didn't hop like a rabbit, he *ran*. His once long ears were shorter, and his bobbly tail was trying to wag.

'He loved your food, Mr Pattacake,' said Katy,
bending down to stroke Treacle, who purred loudly.
'But he's acting more like a dog than a rabbit. I like dogs,
but I preferred my rabbit. He's more like a doggit now.'

Treacle didn't like dogs but he didn't mind rabbits. So now he was confused, not knowing whether to spit or not.

'Don't worry, I'll put it right,' said Mr Pattacake, trying to comfort her. He then went home to think about what to do. It was getting very worrying.

'Somehow the pots got mixed up,' he said to Treacle, who hung his head in shame. But it wasn't his fault. After all, cats couldn't read.

Just then, the doorbell rang.

'I'm Mr Martin,' said the man on the doorstep. 'I gave my goldfish your new Fish's Feast, and now he… well, you'd better come and see for yourself.'

Mr Pattacake and Treacle followed Mr Martin to his house, anticipating the worst once again. Mr Pattacake gasped when he saw a shattered fish bowl on the floor, and a puddle of water surrounding it.

'This is Goldy,' said Mr Martin, pointing at the creature on the soaked carpet. 'But something has happened to him since he ate your fish food.'

Something had happened to him indeed.

He was still gold, at least, but now he had completely outgrown his bowl and seemed to be able to breathe air. What's more, he had grown little legs and was hopping about all over the floor, his little nose twitching. He was still mostly covered in scales, but he had grown a fluffy tail, and long furry ears were sprouting out of his head.

'Oh dear,' said Mr Pattacake in disbelief. 'What a curious creature.'

'Yes,' said Mr Martin. 'But I want my goldfish back. You have to do something about it, Mr Pattacake. He keeps digging holes in the garden.'

'Don't worry, I'll put it right,' said Mr Pattacake. But now he was getting more and more worried. *How* was he going to put it right?

By now he knew that he could expect a couple more complaints, and sure enough, a letter arrived the next day. Usually, a letter caused great excitement, as it often meant a new job for him and Treacle. But this time he opened it with dread, not wanting to find out what was inside.

'Dear Mr Pattacake,' he read, cautiously:

'You have to do something. Ever since I gave some of your Snake's Supper to my snake, he's been acting really strangely.'

When they arrived at the man's house, Treacle backed away into a corner as soon as he saw the snake. He had never seen a snake before, but he was sure that they shouldn't look like this one did.

Mr Pattacake had never been up close to a snake before either, but one thing he knew for sure, was that they didn't have legs. No snake had legs. If they did, they were a lizard, not a snake. Snakes wriggled and slithered. This one walked. It walked with its tail in the air. A fluffy tail. Also, Mr Pattacake knew that snakes hissed. That was the only sound they made. They certainly did *not* meow.

'My goodness!' said Mr Pattacake in shock.

'You may well say that,' agreed the man. 'I have studied snakes all my life. I'm a herpetologist, and I have never seen anything like this before. How did you do it, Mr Pattacake?'

'Well, I… I think things got a little bit mixed up in the kitchen,' he said, sheepishly, glaring at Treacle, who retreated further into the corner shamefacedly.

'You mean cat food was accidentally put into the pots for snake food? How interesting. I'd like to know what was in the food, Mr Pattacake. This is amazing. It's a scientific breakthrough!'

Mr Pattacake smiled for the first time in ages. At last, a pet owner who was not angry about the changes in their pet, but was actually *interested* in them.

'I'll give you the recipe,' he said, feeling more cheerful.

'But...' said the man. 'I do want my snake back though.'

'Don't worry, I'll put it right,' said Mr Pattacake, nodding as he and Treacle left.

There was really no point in setting his imagination to work until the last pet owner contacted him, so he waited.

The next day, the doorbell rang again.

On the step stood a small boy holding a birdcage. He blinked up at Mr Pattacake from under his mop of unruly brown hair.

'Look what your food has done to Tweety,' he said, holding up the heavy cage with great difficulty.

'Come in,' said Mr Pattacake, before even looking into the cage. 'I've been expecting you.'

He helped the boy lift the birdcage onto the worktop in the kitchen.

Inside was what could only be described as a *snudgie*. It had once been a blue budgie but most of its feathers had turned into scales, and its feet had completely disappeared. It opened its mouth and a long forked tongue flicked out.

Of course, it could no longer sit on its perch, but instead wriggled along the bottom of the cage. When it tried to tweet, only a soft hissing sound came out.

Treacle didn't like the creature at all. It didn't look anything like that naughty budgie which had refused to leave the kitchen when Mr Pattacake was making the food. That one had been green.

Then something stirred in the back of his mind. What had that green budgie been up to? The look on its face had reminded him of that sneaky tortoiseshell cat, Naughty Tortie, who he hadn't seen for a while.

'I want my budgie back, Mr Pattacake,' pleaded the boy. 'My mum doesn't like snakes.'

'Don't worry, I'll put it right,' said Mr Pattacake with a smile. Now was the time. All the pet owners had finally contacted him so he had to use his imagination to put the pets back as they were. It would need some extra strong ingredients.

Not only had the pet owners complained to Mr Pattacake, but they had all gone round to **ANiMEALS** to complain there too. The manager was almost exploding with rage.

'I've had hundreds of pet owners queuing up outside to make a complaint,' he said, waving his hand to indicate how long the queue had been. 'And they turned up with a very strange variety of animals. Who is responsible for this mistake?'

Mr Pattacake looked at Treacle, who thought that it wasn't very fair that he was being blamed. Everyone knew that cats couldn't read. And anyway, he had the feeling that someone else was responsible. He stared back at Mr Pattacake.

'Ah,' said Mr Pattacake. 'I may be partly to blame for not checking the labels, but I do believe that there has been some mischief going on here.'

He too was remembering the budgie who had refused to leave. He now remembered seeing, out of the corner of his eye, the budgie with a pot lid in his beak. He'd been too busy to think anything of it at the time.

'It doesn't matter whose fault it was now. All I know is that you must put it right, Mr Pattacake,' said the manager of ANiMEALS, sternly. 'The food was a great success, but we must make sure that the right pets get the right food this time.'

'So it was that mischievous budgie all along,' said Mr Pattacake when the manager had left. 'He swapped the lids and then I didn't check. So,

The Dog's Dinner went into the pot for rabbits.

The Cat's Casserole went into the snake food.

The Rabbit's Rations went into the fish food.

The Bird's Breakfast went into the cat's pot.

The Fish's Feast went into the dog's food.

And the Snake's Supper went into the bird's food.

Oh dear!'

Mr Pattacake thought and thought. How was he going to put this right? He really had to stretch his imagination. His big chef's hat wobbled as his brain whirred inside his head. Never had it had to work so hard before.

He thought…

And thought…

And thought…

And then he had a brilliant idea.

'Yippee!' He did his silly dance to show his excitement.

Soon, he and Treacle had the six pans out again.

This time, however, Mr Pattacake made sure that *he* checked the labels, and no little budgie, or anyone else for that matter, was allowed in his kitchen while he worked.

Just to make sure the recipes would work, he added some extra ingredients:

In the Dog's Dinner, he added a little piece of *bark*.

In the Cat's Casserole, he added a spoonful of *Mews-li*.

In the Rabbit's Rations, he added a handful of *hops*.

In the Bird's Breakfast, he added a dead *fly*.

He weighed the Fish's Feast very carefully on the *scales*.

And cooked the Snake's Supper until it *hissed*.

Then they took the whole lot back to **ANiMEALS** where the manager invited all the pet owners back, as well as their pets, to feed them the correct food.

The queue went right round the block and it took the whole day to feed each animal with the correct food, a process very carefully supervised by Mr Pattacake.

Then all they could do was to wait patiently.

Gradually things began to happen.

Benny, the dog, shook off his scales and barked excitedly at his owner, who looked relieved to have a normal dog again. But Benny absolutely *refused* to get in the bath to wash off the slimy pond weed!

Fluffy, the cat, became fluffy again, and stopped trying to fly.

Bounce, the rabbit, hopped about, twitching his little nose with familiar vigour.

Goldy, the goldfish, had a new bowl, and as he became smaller and scalier, his owner popped him back into the water, just before his fluffy tail disappeared.

The herpetologist reminded Mr Pattacake about the promised recipe, and then he happily wound his furless snake around his neck and went home.

Tweety's owner popped the budgie back into its cage once its legs had grown back so it could sit on its perch. The budgie began to preen its newly restored feathers.

Mr Pattacake and Treacle looked very closely at Tweety but could see no resemblance to that naughty *green* budgie who had mixed up the lids. The budgie that had reminded them of the troublesome cat, Naughty Tortie.

They knew they would have to watch out for that mischievous cat in future, whatever animal her spirit chose to inhabit.